THE LOST NOTEBOOK

THE
LOST
NOTEBOOK

by

JOHN MONTAGUE

who was so angry about those Amendments; fa Tom Halpin who grew through it all: John

With Illustrations by
JOHN VERLING

THE MERCIER PRESS
CORK & DUBLIN

THE MERCIER PRESS LIMITED
4 Bridge St, Cork
24 Lower Abbey Street, Dublin 1

Text © John Montague 1987
Illustrations © John Verling 1987

British Library Cataloguing in Publication Data
Montague, John *1929–*
    The lost notebook.
    I. Title
    823'.914[F]   PR6063. 05

    ISBN 0-85342-831-X
    ISBN 0-85342-832-8 Pbk

This book is published with the financial assistance of the Arts Council/
An Chomhairle Ealaíon, Ireland.

Thanks to Desmond O'Grady for the use of his quotation on page 11,
and other felicities, and *Exile* (Toronto) where the first version of this story
appeared. Ellen Beardsley and Susan Lederman also cast a warm eye and
Val Bogan made clean copy.

Contents

For Francis Stuart

Pilgrim's Pad

I

It was a makeshift Notebook of the kind I am writing
in now, small, neat, vellum finish, an ordinary writing
pad of the kind one might buy in any shabby little street
corner stationer among the sweeties, perhaps with a
wolfhound and round tower on its cover. I probably got
it in Dublin before I left, but why I carried it with me
through Europe that summer I don't really know. I was
never one for writing home, though I probably managed
an occasional note, to stave the anxiety of my elders,
who had never travelled outside Ireland except via the
emigrant boat, ollagoaning, lamenting, all the way.

Besides, my wanderings were now accepted in the
family with something near fatalism, as a youthful,
probably pagan ritual, leading me far from 'mother
church, motherland and mother'. I do remember send-
ing a triumphant postcard from Padua to my mother,
who had a great devotion to St Anthony, among many
other saints, of course. And another from Assisi,
Giotto's *St Francis Preaching to the Birds.* It was always
my casuistical contention that Europe was packed with
shrines, where the saints we heard of in church had
lived and died. And now the half century, 1950, had
been proclaimed by the Pope himself as a Holy Year,
Anno Santo, so that I could present myself as a pilgrim,
ardent to reach the holy door.

It was also my twenty-first year, and in the absence

of any official recognition of my coming of age, I had planned and was now giving myself a kind of *Wander-jahre*, to assuage my hunger for all sorts of experience which I felt lacking in my native land. It was a rhythm that had become part of my life. I would reach out as far as I could on the continent, for as long as I could manage, and then return slowly, usually through repatriation, to Ireland. There I would manage to survive, buoyed up by all I had seen and heard, until I had to hit the road again. Years later such forays abroad would become part of ordinary Irish student life, but in my urgency I was something of a pioneer, a new kind of Hibernian savage, invading the continent in search of art and love, *Peregrinus Hibernicus*, a horn-mad celibate with a bright red comb and a roving eye.

It was a different Europe, of course, not criss-crossed with charter planes, not crammed with package tours and student fares. Then you made your way slowly, wearily, by boat and bus and train, waking gradually to some new excitement, like walking out into the aquatic bustle of Venice from San Lucia Station. Or cycling through the French countryside, surprised by lines of vines, the thick rustling of maize, bulbous red tomatoes, a glowing Van Gogh field of *tournesol*. Or the straight line through Paris from the *Gare du Nord* to the Youth Hostel at *Porte d'Orleans*; it made my non-linear intelligence boggle. The fierce roar of the *autoroute du Sud*, thronged with long distance lorries, trailers and family cars, was still far away, in the crowded future.

I suppose I was planning to keep a *Journal:* Gide had

recently received the Nobel Prize and introspection was fashionable. But I did nothing as systematic as that for now only fragments from that summer float up before me; a curious visit to the headquarters of the Soviet Zone in Vienna; a night sleeping in a field outside Bologna, waking wet with morning dew; a zealous perusal of the subtleties of Sienese Art, trying to distinguish between all that gold and slanting eyes. Piecing the jigsaw, I realise that it was a bewildering but necessary summer of growth, a preparation for something unknown, some sensuous epiphany.

But back to the Notebook, that small white block of writing paper that survived intact in my rucksack through all those months. It survived longer than that, and I may still unearth it, but as my wandering approach suggests, I may not want to: it could betray and embarrass me. It already has, which is part of my story, a coda or tail to my lagging kite.

The main part takes place in Florence, *Firenze*, where I had dropped off again on my way back from Rome. Yes, I had made it to the Holy City, all the way down the spine of Italy from Venice, my beard now red and ragged, my arms stippled with freckles. And, yes, I did visit the four Basilicas, and saw the Pope being ferried on the *Sedia Gestatoria*. I was within spitting distance of the pale bespectacled Pacelli, *Pio Dodicesimo*, because I was there as part of an official delegation, the International Conference on Catholic Cinema, to give its full, sonorous title.

That was because of my work on *The Catholic Eagle* at

home in Dublin as a film critic. So I led a double life, nights in the Youth Hostel, a hectic barracks on the outskirts of Rome, where a late bus dropped me off in the evenings, and days as a delegate at the conference, sporting my one suit, for official meetings and at receptions. A famous Irish actor was attending it also, using the trip as an excuse for a holiday. And he was very friendly to me, bringing me everywhere with him like a mascot, deferring to my unfledged but extreme opinions in literature and art, my wild plans. Together we gaped at the ceiling of the Sistine Chapel, loitered through the endless rooms of the Vatican Gallery. Then back to his central hotel in the evenings, where we would have cherries soaked in red wine on the terrace. And if I was lucky, he would bring me with him afterwards to a *trattoria*, my one meal of the day. Between the heat and the wine I barely made it back.

But let the journey curve back to Florence, through the white splendour of Rome's new railway station, after the conference was over, and my generous actor friend had flown away. I had stayed in a pilgrim's hostel on the way down, and been thrown out for returning late. I tried to explain to the priest in charge that I was trying to combine sightseeing with pilgrimage but the philistine refused to see my point. So this time I made my way to the youth hostel, another large, thronged, happy building: the night burned with light and voices until well after midnight. And during the day I continued my exploration of Florence, from Ghiberti's Baptistery doors to the Roman theatre at

Fiesole, where I sat stunned in the afternoon sunlight.

My problem was time: three days was the limit in any hostel and though I doubled it by hitchhiking to Siena and back, the time was approaching when I would have to leave. And I had only begun to understand the glory that was Florence! Earnest, intent, insufferable, I was determined to be an apostle of art, a martyr, if necessary, in the cause of beauty! But there seemed no way that I could simply stay on.

I shared the washing up with an English speaking South African, who was also on his European year before he went home to take over the family business. He was stocky, neat and slow spoken, but perhaps because we were opposites, we made a good enough team. He knew nothing about art, except that he should know about it, so he probed me for the little I had found out for myself, with a battered copy of an old-fashioned guidebook in my rucksack, which I promised to leave him. There was a Victorian earnestness about Pieter; he probably disapproved of such paganism, but it had to be seen.

So on my last morning he followed me through the city centre, for a farewell look and then bought me a light lunch, a *panino* and a glass of wine, in a *trattoria*. We sat in the cool, listening for the rustle of the bead curtain as chatty Italians flowed in and out. All this richness and colour was about to leave my life; my rucksack was stowed under the table and I would shortly be tramping towards the station. I was sullen and down in the mouth, a poor companion.

Sympathetic to my silence, he suggested that I should wait for the night train, and come with him to meet a very strange young girl he had found himself beside in a queue at the American Express. 'Very strange,' he emphasised, in his clipped tones, under his little moustache. 'You know how Americans are,' he said, 'very young but very loud. But she did ask me round, God knows what for. Says she's a painter and I told her I'd met this young poet chap from Ireland, who can't stop talking about painting. Like to know what you'd make of her. Really would.' He sounded uneasy, still terse, but tense, for some reason.

So instead of the afternoon train to Paris, or hitch-hiking the dusty fringe of some high road, I found myself squatting on the stone floor of a small studio, at the feet of a young American girl. She was quite young, a little older than me, pretty but, by my provincial standards, shameless, as she twiddled her brightly painted toes right under our noses. Clearly, my South African friend bored her, but she was lonely and wanted to speak English. I had never really known anyone like her, with a halter holding her already overflowing breasts, and shorts riding carelessly high on tanned legs. However, I *had* met her once before. . .

II

I had met her in the Uffizi Gallery. Since I didn't have enough money to eat at midday I had taken to staying in a gallery through lunchtime, to avoid the sight of people eating; as well as to increase my knowledge of painting, of course. Trying to stave your hunger by staring at the details of master works is an interesting exercise in mortification, especially in the heat of the day; what I had developed was a restless and ambulatory form of the *siesta*, like a mad monk on hunger-strike outside the door of a refectory. Down in the Piazza della Signoria, happy tourists were tucking in, under gaily coloured awnings. If I looked towards Rivoire or Ruffino, my eyes stuck out on stalks, so I stared at the paintings, as if through a magnifying glass.

On bad days, all still lives were banned. Glorious pyramids of ruddy-cheeked fruit; vermilion cherries; green, black and purple grapes; soft furred peaches; on my imagination's palate they burst endlessly. Streams of juice ran down my cheeks, seeds stuck to be sucked in my teeth until in the intensity of my hallucination I ran from the room. Sticks of bread doubly disturbed me. Thank God I was in Florence and not in some Dutch museum, with rich ruddy sides of beef, freshly hung game or venison, the saliva-raising sight of a Breughel village feast, full bellies and distended codpieces, rich food *and* lusty love afterwards. The worst I had to face was Caravaggio's *Adolescent Bacchus*, his cheeks already ruddy with the wine fumes, a piled bowl of fruit before him to gorge on.

Sometimes I tried to assuage one hunger by another, spending a long time, for example, in the cool decorum of the Botticelli room. Venus rising from her half shell, a strand of flaxen hair held demurely over her *pudenda*, her visage pensive; she was as mysterious and refreshing as an early morning by the sea. Luckily, I had not yet become an amateur of the oyster or *coquilles Saint Jacques* or that half shell might have been another source of temptation.

I was especially drawn to the room with the great Titians; large sensuous females at ease in their nudity, as leisurely and complete as domestic animals. The reclining *Venus of Urbino* also had a hand over her gently swelling belly to cover her thatch, but the eye slid down that listless, boneless arm to join the fingers; it was a gently inviting slope, not a protective pudic gesture. And her soft, brown eyes and coiled auburn hair seemed to gather one in to her rich nakedness, to lie beside her on that tousled linen bedspread where she had drowsed so long, be it only as the pampered lapdog curled beside her crossed calves.

But I would have to avoid even them if I had had no breakfast. The lightheadedness of hunger can lead to extreme forms of lust and sometimes I was less aware of the luminous Venetian tonality of the paintings, less inclined to compare them with Bellini and Giorgione in

their use of colour, than overcome by their sulky phys-ical presence. A scraggy frustrated Irish adolescent, I gaped at them hungrily, like the cats thrown in the Colosseum, and could hardly hold myself back from leaping through the canvas to bite, even slice a voluptu-ous, golden haunch. Blake's 'lineaments of gratified desire' I thought, as my stomach growled. Would I ever know such satisfaction?

Gazing at them I realised that someone was watching them and me. It was a young blonde with brown tanned skin and ice blue eyes like the corn maiden of some Northern tale. With her cascade of hair, and her slender but full hipped figure, she looked as if she had stepped down from the frame of a painting! She had a red belt tucked tightly around her waist and wore bright red slippers of a kind I had seen in the market behind the Duomo. They seemed to flicker in and out under her light skirt to match her impatience, as she sized me up before speaking: 'Gee, I wish I could lay on the paint like that,' she said in a nasal American voice, almost a whine. 'What's this guy's name again?'

Grateful for the excuse to show off my knowledge, I gabbled about Titian, *Tiziano Vecelli*, and his part in the Venetian High Renaissance. She listened with what I hoped was interest, contemplating me with her express-ionless eyes. Then she turned on her heel and left with a parting shot that stung: 'Thanks for the lecture, Mick.' She made it sound like *hick*, an insult I knew from my reading. Was it so obvious that I was Irish, a gabbling Paddy? 'I have to run to the American Express. See you around sometime, maybe.'

The last word was emphasised, *may-be* drawn out with scorn until it seemed to rhyme with *unlikely* or not if I see you first, *buddy*. So I had bored her. I watched her tight little bum swagger down the corridor away from me, the lift of each hip a gesture of disdain. Or so I thought, looking hopelessly after the first really pretty girl I had spoken to in months. . .

And yet here I was speaking to her again, my head only a short distance from her warm brown legs and knees. And she was finding me amusing, or at least less boring than my South African friend, whom she teased relentlessly. 'Are they really all like you down there? We've got blacks, too, you know, but you sound like some fruity mixture of British stuck up and Georgia cracker when you talk about them. Let 'em be, they can't be as bad as you sound. Bet your women like them – they got the old jelly roll.' And she waggled her bottom on the chair, above him.

Pieter did not know what to make of her as she rambled on about race and colour and sex: I gathered she was from New York and had definite views about all three. For the moment, I decided to agree with her about them all, if it insured my being close to her for even a while longer. *Maybe God will be good*, I thought with a mixture of faith, hope and lechery.

He decided to master his irritation by showing that he did not take her seriously; she was too young.

'I think you are just a naughty girl,' he said indulgently, waving at her, like a swagger stick, the short ruler he had found on the floor near an easel. She went off into wild giggles.

'Don't you shake your little stick at me, Mr Man,' she said in what I recognised as a parody of a Southern accent. Then when he began to look not only puzzled, but angry: 'Haven't you read Freud, you nuthead? You're wagging that stick at me because you want to spank or fuck me, but you don't dare ask, do you, you silly racist prick?'

Raging, thin-lipped, my South African friend·rose to go. He expected me to come with him, but I had been explaining to her earlier about having to leave the hostel. Watching me hesitate, she saw a chance to hurt him still more.

'Why don't you park your rucksack here? You look too young to be out but you can't be dumber than him. If you are, you can always just sleep on the floor for a few days.'

With a weak attempt at a chilly look, the South African left and Wandy Lang and I stared at each other. That hot July night in Florence, I slept in her narrow bed, beneath her easel.

American Express

If she does not come, my heart stands still:
Instead of summer, winter in a bound.
And if she comes, my golden girl,
Where do I stand? I die as well.

III

And I spent the rest of the month in that cot, except when we quarrelled, and I slept on the stone floor in my sleeping bag. A strange duel took place in that hot narrow cell, on the fourth floor of an old Florentine house; a duel of unequals. There was my timidity, so much a product of my time and place, our forgotten island on the sheltered edge of Europe which had largely avoided the war. And her avid American greed for experience, spoilt child of a rich, but predatory world. We were both looking for something, but she expected it, I vainly hoped for it; the lately victorious and the colonial victim were bound to be at loggerheads.

She wouldn't help me, at first, during those long, hot nights: every move was up to me. And my knowledge of female anatomy was restricted to picture gazing; lacking sisters or adventurous girl friends, I was a typical product of an Irish clerical education, eager but ignorant. Sometimes I made it to the magic centre, but often I fumbled, grappling blindly in that airless tiny oven of a room, where our bodies stuck together like stamps. And every time I fell back, she made sure it hurt.

'I'm not going to help you. You're all that I hate, kids that are clumsy and stupid. Why should I show you the works, you little Irish Catholic prick. Fuck you—'

At first, I tried to give some smart answer like, 'but that's what I want you to do.' But after tirades like these I usually lay awake, silent, hurt, still hoping. And she would rise in the morning, blithe as if nothing had happened. Then we would go out to take a *caffe latte* together, inside the bead curtain if it was too hot, on the sidewalk if there was a cool breeze. And then we would begin our day together, which was usually easier than the night, with her painting, and me trying to write.

And as the days passed I began to hope against hope that I might be able to please her. She was my meal ticket, of course, and the unsubtle art of freeloading was one I had already learnt a little of in the drab school of Dublin pub life in the late 1940s. But I also believed dimly in my mystic mission as a young poet, and around us lay all the ingredients for an idyll. With that impossible mixture of hunger and idealism, I set out to try and understand this ferocious young woman whom fate had flung directly across my pilgrim path.

IV

Wandy Lang was pretty, rich but wild and clawing as a lost alley-cat. She was not looking for the way out of an Irish Catholic childhood, stumbling towards fulfilment, but seeking something that would anneal, annul the empty ache that was already eating her. Somewhere along the line, someone or something had hurt her, in a more drastic way than all the pious regulations of my education. Or perhaps the combination of money and freedom that her background seemed to offer her was only an illusion, that left her still empty and angry? Whatever the reason, she was trying to work it out, in her own strange way, far from her compatriots, in a loneliness that somehow resembled my own Quixotic quest. But worse; she was American and buying: I had nothing to sell.

Perhaps sex would help? She certainly seemed to have tried it, to judge by her wild language, her ceaseless use of words like *prick* and *ass* and *cunt*. In theory I was all for calling a spade a bloody shovel but to hear her shapely young mouth spew swearwords scandalised me. When she was angry it rang like a litany, a litany of desecration, of blasphemy, but also of loss and longing, if I had been able to hear its dark rhythms.

But now her 'thing' was art. Her elder brother was a painter, whom she admired blindly, and wanted to emulate. Although she emphasised, he would be disgusted if he knew she was daring to paint, herself. He had always discouraged her because he was a real painter, a serious painter, like Paul Klee, or 'Pete' Mondrian, the biggest modern painter, who had replaced nature. Did I know his tree series?

I had never heard of Mondrian, and I certainly couldn't judge the kind of painting she was doing, carefully planned with an architecture of lines, constructed with the ruler the South African had wagged at her, and then intently filled in squares, triangles and lozenges of colour. But she really worked: after breakfast, she set up her easel in the middle of the room to catch what little light came through our open window, and with bare midriff and loosely tied hair, she pointed herself at the canvas silently for hours. Heat flared up the Florentine sky with its glimpses of red tiled roofs, the ochre façade of a high building. Her hair would tumble sweatily down, her forehead bead, until she unconsciously untied her blouse and stood bare-breasted before the canvas, like a defiant young Amazon. Now that I know more of painters and painting, I know that she was trying to imitate somebody, her brother probably and his peers, in a pathetic parody of their intent preoccupation.

While she sweated before her easel, I tried to write poems. But it was too hot to concentrate properly and I was so obsessed with her presence before me in the small room that I could think only of one subject. Particularly when she stood naked to the waist before the easel, hair rippling down to her hips, oblivious of

my surreptitious glances. I tried to write little poems about her, in praise of her ripe body, its mixture of sensuous yet childish boldness. They were Chinese lyrics, in the style of Pound, whose incarceration had made him an idol for the Irish young: a prisoner for the cause.

> Her blond hair pours
> down her studded spine;
> bare to the waist,
> she stands, my girl.

Surrounded by the shy lasses of my country, I had touched, but rarely seen breasts. In Ireland, it was the blind leading the blind, but with Wandy I could stare and stare endlessly, feasting my eyes on those mysterious forbidden globes before I began to try and net them in words.

> How warm her white breasts!
> Two bowls of cream with
> Her nipples, bright cherries.

Such naive tenderness! But the ardour of that young man in the Florentine heat reaches out for my indulgence across three decades. We were a pair, a team, in our blundering ambition; as she dragged her brush across an area of canvas, or peered before adding a touch of colour, I tried to study her as a painter might, my first life class, but a very modern one, for I was painting a standing nude who was trying to paint an abstract; a nearly Cubist vision of reality!

As she works, she pouts,
Her face is young, serious.
Her eyes, sharp blue.

And so forth. One day she looked over my shoulder. 'Hey there,' she exclaimed, 'you make me sound nice.' And she looked at me with warm, surprised eyes. Then she leaned over and gave me a quick kiss, the first she had ever given me in daylight.

From then on, the Notebook followed us everywhere, to museums, restaurants, cafes, sometimes churches. She had taken to drawing in it, wild, impulsive scrawls to go with the poems. Clearly, I had found the way to her heart, for even in bed she began to ease up, relaxing her guard to the point where she seemed almost tender. And I was beginning to improve a little, learning how to please, to be a lover, although she was already so precocious that I lagged far behind, a blundering innocent, who had to be taught how to kiss properly. She taught me other tricks, things that I only half understood, bending her urgent body like a bow, as she searched avidly for the next sensation; coiling her spine, like a cat, in shudders of self delight.

Somehow, desperately, I felt that this was wrong, that wild experiment should be the joyous fruit of love, not its budding point. But who was I to argue with her? She already knew so much more than I did about the mechanics of sex that our couplings were bound to seem clumsy and ludicrous, forcing her into the incongruous role of the older woman, the instructress of male naïveté. 'No, touch me here. Higher up. And keep that

other hand down. And slowly, gently, women like to be stroked.' Or, in another mood: 'Don't tell me you never did it like this! That's the best way to penetrate, to get it deep. Look at the animals: I thought you said you were brought up on a farm. Some cowboy you are.' And when I was spent, her hand or rasping tongue could reach out to revive me, rise me.

I did my best, or thought I did, to follow her urgent instructions. And she tried to control, restrain whatever irritation my incompetence caused her, compared to her previous male friends. Whoever had taught her the erotic arts had done it well, for there seemed to be little that she did not know, taking baths together like mad children, moving the bed until it was under the wall mirror, dancing together naked, before we slid to the floor, or bed. And for a while we seemed to enter into, at least hover near, the sweet conspiracy of lovers, although such words of endearment were not part of her harsh vocabulary. The widow next door, for instance, was shocked to discover that there was a young man staying with Wandy, a half-naked savage with red hair. As we shared a lavatory on the landing it was difficult to avoid meeting but she would lower her eyes when she saw us passing. And once Wandy came to the door to kiss me, forgetting to cover her breasts, rather not bothering, the dark, startled Italian woman crossed herself, rattling the crucifix on her black dress.

V

To be twenty one, to have a girlfriend – a mistress! – and to have the run of Florence; it seemed like the fulfilment of the dream that had lured me all the way from Ireland. I had padded down its narrow streets for more than a week before I met her and now she had given me a month's reprieve, with the added pleasure of being a guide to a beautiful young woman. For she seemed to have lived in Florence as if it were any raw American city, seeing, sensing its quality without understanding it. She knew it was a place to be but why wasn't clear to her. So the little I knew I lavished on her while I kept boning up more in the British Institute library, so as to impress her, like I had tried that first time in the Uffizi. Laying my small treasures of knowledge before her, like a faithful spaniel, I was often oblivious to the ironies of the situation, as when I introduced her to the Fra Angelicos in the Convent of San Marco.

The first time we got turned away because of the shorts and halter she was wearing. But we came back and in those cool cloisters, shaded by flowerbeds and Lebanese cedars, we saw the fruits of the saintly painter's meditation, a guide to prayer, a fervent hymn to the glory of a Christian God. A long fingered St Dominic clasping, embracing, the Cross down which ran the ruby rivulets of Christ's passion, the delicate dialogue of the *Annunciation*, the blue of the Virgin's cloak and the multicoloured wings of the Angel Gabriel, the rainbow tinted dance of the Elect in his *Last Judgement;* I could not help but hush before such feeling. These were not the gaudy images of my Ulster Catholic childhood; they seemed to breathe a mystical aroma, as light and radiant as the wing of a butterfly. Somewhere in me my fading belief stirred, the very faith I felt I had to disdain in order to live.

But for Wandy they were only pretty geegaws, relics from a world long dead, inspired by emotions that no one would ever need again. Emerging from that rich silence she enquired plaintively: 'They're pretty colours but why did he have to waste so much time painting virgins and saints and old stuff like that? We've left all that behind now. My brother says real painting should only be about itself.'

So I brought her to the Medici Palace, also built by Michelozzo. For me it was a Poundian paradigm of creative order, the walls where the Medici, those munificent mafiosi, lived and lavished their wealth. They were all there in the ornate frescoes of Gozzoli, Emperors and Patriarchs invited from the East to join them in a stately procession through the landscape of Tuscany. It might be based on the Magi but the emphasis was on earthly glory, clothes stiff with ornament, gloriously caparisoned horses. She looked for a long time at a handsome young man, astride a leopard. ' I like him,' she said and when I explained that he was the brother of Lorenzo the Magnificent she added: 'he's as cute as my brother,' and smacked her lips.

She went silent at last in the Medici crypt before the unfinished torsos of Michelangelo. She lingered before *Dusk* and *Dawn*, froze like a gundog before *Day*, fighting to free himself, large muscled and intent, from cloudy matter. But it was the ambiguous, sombre figure of *Night*, its large breasts and bent head, with sad, brooding eyelids, which finally got to her. 'Jee-sus,' she exclaimed, 'I thought these were done by a man. He must have been pretty lonely to feel like that. I didn't know you could get that deep down chipping a stone. It's as black as the Blues.'

She tried to thank me, in her own way, for trying to show her so much, for sharing. Day after day passed without a dispute, and in bed at night she was, if not submissive, more subdued in her demands, less insulting in her remarks on my performance. Something akin to peace began to grow between us. Surprised by beauty daily, we made our fumbling efforts to create it ourselves, and afterwards we strolled by the Arno, holding hands as the sun lit the red of the roofs, the yellow brown of the turbid river.

On every walk we seemed to discover something, a lovely Venus in the Boboli Gardens, *The Deposition of Christ from the Cross* by Pontormo, in a church near the Ponte Vecchio. And if I didn't know about Mondrian, I had heard of Masaccio, Big Tom, and led her to obscure churches where the walls were covered with his work; Adam and Eve fleeing from paradise, his

head bowed, her hands shading her body from a relentless red angel. This time she did not complain but admired the treatment of the subject. After all, Florentine painting was a disciplined art, with the kind of geometry of perspective that she was looking for in modern art; colour called to colour, shape balanced shape.

From the blue and white cherubs of Della Robbia to the flower covered meadows of Botticelli's *Primavera*, I tried to offer it all to her, watching as she watched, ignorant but excited, a child gazing at a galaxy of dazzling stars. Back in the Botticelli room she danced for joy, like the three graces in their transparent veils, and when I told her that Venus rising from her shell was Simonetta, the beloved of the young man riding the Gozzoli leopard, she clapped her hands like someone listening to a nursery story for the first time. Especially when I added: 'she makes me think a bit of you, when you look thoughtful, with your hair down.' And danced for me again, shyly moving her lissom body to the inaudible rhythms of the paintings. My heart was in my mouth as I watched, her graceful heel and instep echoing the flaxen haired Florentine beauties of the wall. And then she bowed, and broke into a phrase of Italian I did not know: 'Mi piace molto ballare,' *I really love to dance.*

When she had first come to Florence she had tried to learn Italian from a family to whom she had an introduction, again arranged by her brother. Now she asked them if she could bring me along and told them proudly

that I was a poet. With the deference of older Euro-
peans to any mention of high art I was received,
scraggy and sweating in my single suit, as if I were the
real thing, instead of a gaping novice. Red wine flowed,
pastascuitta, and liquid syllables of Italian that sounded
splendid even if I only dimly understood. And when
our host began to quote Dante, with all the sonorous
intimacy of a Florentine, I responded with Yeats, boom
answering boom, like church bells ringing across the
city. For the first time I heard those great lines des-
cribing the plight of the doomed lovers, Paola and
Francesca, their adulterous eyes meeting over a beloved
book:

> When we read how a lover slaked his drouth
> upon those long desired lips, then he
> who never shall be separated from me
>
> all trembling, kissed my eager mouth.

and I countered with:

> Beloved, may your sleep be sound
> that have found it where you fed.

Our host's wife beamed. Wandy beamed. And when
they wouldn't let us leave after lunch but ushered us
for the siesta into a small white room with a real bed
with laundered linen sheets, Wandy was beside herself
with girlish delight. 'They must think we're married or
engaged or something.' And she blushed. And in those
cool white sheets we made love with no preconcep-
tions, no inhibitions, sweetly, tenderly, turning to each
other with muted cries of delight, nibbling and hugging

like children before we started again, our lips still joined by a light skein of kisses. That afternoon was her richest gift to me, a glimpse of near ecstasy, of the sensuous fulfilment I longed for in my damp, distant island. And like all such moments it had a scent of permanence, a small addition to the sum of sweetness in the world. Finally she fell asleep, her blonde head resting on my numbed arm, in total ease.

In the crook of my arm
my love's head rests;
in each breath
I taste her trust.

VI

That was our high point, the crest of the wave. But it couldn't last, it seems; we soon plunged down. Already that evening, as we stumbled home, she had begun to turn sour. Between the harmony of the afternoon and the airless heat of her little room, the dinginess of the narrow iron bed, was a distance she couldn't, wouldn't cross. When she was in that mood she had to yield to every caprice, however hurtful. There is a certain kind of character that needs to strike out, to wound, and if the victim cares enough to complain, all the worse for them. I fought back at first, but when I found that not only was it useless but it made things much worse, I lapsed into stricken silence.

As she did also, except that she could dredge depths of melancholy, of sadness that I had never seen in any one before. As the heat grew daily, we took to going to a suburban swimming pool, to escape from the baking claustrophobia of her little studio. The pool was a gaudy, massive imitation of a Roman Baths, the kind of official architecture that flourished during the Mussolini period. Like most young Americans, Wandy Lang could swim like a fish, used to pools and swimming classes from her infancy. And like most young Irishmen, I had not been properly taught, and floundered nervously at the shallow end, despising my own pale freckled skin.

And for most Italian men the Baths was a theatre to strut, and show off their wares. They wore crotch tight swimming trunks and as they looked at her they stroked themselves, openly. And she seemed to like it, to welcome it; there were very few other women there and she had their full attention. Especially as she wore the first bikini I had ever seen, exposing her acorn brown navel, that cup from which I had newly learnt to drink. When she struck into the water they dipped and dived around her, like dolphins. And when she stretched down to cool, they paraded about her like distended fighting cocks. As I climbed gingerly in, at the shallow or child's end, to practise the breast stroke, they raced past, showering me with spray.

Humiliated, I sat with a towel around my burnt shoulders and tried to contemplate the water, as a kind of exercise. Water in swimming pools changes appearance more than in any other container. The sea always seems to be the same colour but in a pool water is controlled and its rhythms reflect not only the sky but because of its transparency, the depth of the water as well. If the surface is almost still and there is a strong sun, a dancing line with all the colours of the spectrum will appear anywhere. I tried to share the intensity of my contemplation with Wandy, appealing to her pictorial sense, but she only grunted, as if I were a boring schoolboy, distracting her from the company of grown-ups. My appeal to our artistic comradeship was in vain.

One afternoon I could take no more, and tried to protest to Wandy, where she lay on the edge of the pool, holding her shoulders and breasts up to the sun, then untying her bikini halter to turn, like Saint Lawrence on his gridiron, her breasts downwards. This move always delighted her audience, especially as she did it slowly, to let them feast their eyes on her body. I could neither stand nor understand it: I had begun to love that body, and that she should let them gape and slaver over it was beyond me.

'Shut up, you little puritan,' she snapped back at me, 'just because you can't swim properly you want everyone else to go round hunched up like a cripple. You Irish hate water and sun.' I tried to explain to her that, despite their preening and pushing, her pack of admirers were as frustrated as any Irish provincial. The dark cloud of *la mamma*, as well as holy Mother Church, hung over the home; she was dealing with, teasing, regaling the most conventional males in Europe, with a double set of values, one for their own women, the other for whores and foreigners. Their only experience of sex, outside marriage, would be through the brothel and there money ruled, especially since the dollars of the American army of occupation had ruined the trade. They were full of contempt for foreigners, especially English speaking women on whom they would exact revenge for their humiliation in war. If she did let them near her, they would only despise and drop her.

I was brilliant, I thought, a week's bile exploding in a sermon that surprised even myself. Had the fury of Savonarola, as well as Fra Angelico, infected me after San Marco, where I had visited his tiny cell to

[47]

contemplate on my own? Certainly there was a stench of burning flesh in my speech, a furious rhetoric which wrapped up both her and them, my disappointment at her desertion, my jealousy of their sun warmed maleness. But most of the information was not mine; I had collected it, unconsciously, from film after film, where the tension between the sexes in Italy inflamed the celluloid.

'So you think you know it all,' she said angrily, after we came plodding home from the pool, and began to pull off our heat dampened clothes. She was sitting on the bed, half naked, her skirt already shed to the floor, showing her warm gold thatch. 'Well, I've been fucking since I was sixteen.'

Silence.

'And when did you start?' She answered herself easily. 'You never did, did you? Boy, your country must be backward. You hardly even know where the cunt is. Well, take a good look at it now – for the last time.'

And she lay back, provocatively spreadeagled on the bed, the pretty red shape of her sex, part wound, part flower held open to me. But when I came forward to touch her, she jack-knifed up, laughing and jeering. 'You're not going to use me for your anatomy lesson, brother. If they didn't teach you anything about sex in your country, don't come crying to me. And don't try to tell me about men: I know! You're ashamed of your body, you can't talk. Before I met you, you didn't even know how to clean your foreskin, a real hillbilly. Christ, I don't know what they did to you in your silly schools, but your prick isn't part of you – '

She was right; of course. In school we wore shorts in the showers when we came to hose ourselves down after another sweaty, exhausting game of football, designed to drain us. And yearly we got a lecture on sex from a priest, his face brick red with embarrassment as he tried to explain something that he hardly knew about himself. Our information was garnered furtively, in dirty jokes and stories. Meanwhile the sap rose urgently, blindly in our bodies, adolescents in the charge of celibates, who were as scared as us of that pulsing power, the fermenting energy of sex that couldn't be denied, or channelled for long. But why did she have to mock me; was I not more to be pitied than laughed at, to use our local Ulster expression? Between her early excess of knowledge and my ignorance was a gap that only good will could cross, and Wandy did not see why she should not take charge of my re-education, any more than I was willing to accept her coarseness. Who had initiated her into sex, leaving her with such a mixture of avidity and terrible loneliness?

Meanwhile, we quarrelled, heat, anger, frustration crackling through that narrow room. After each attack, she tried to make it up to me, pleading silently, almost childishly for forgiveness, in little ways that tore my heart. She would bring me a newspaper, for example, or an expensive book from one of the International bookshops. Or a brightly coloured pencil with a rubber on the top; a new fountain pen. But I wouldn't come to the pool again, determined not to be hurt by her, or

those grinning young Italian males, their shorts bulging like nets after a day's catch. I had had enough *machismo* to last me for a lifetime. Instead I trudged to the cool of the British Institute library, absorbing myself again in books, trying to blot out the images of longing and rage that rose in me. It was another version of my artistic hunger strike and about as successful. A sex starved bookworm, I could not, like the common or garden worm, split in two and have sex with my other half.

Suddenly a detail from Berenson's *Florentine Painters of the Renaissance* would come alive and a slender, delicious young body would stand, not before me, but a gaping crowd who devoured her with their eyes. Then I fled to poetry, laboriously trying to decipher the message of the *Duino Elegies*. But then Rilke would betray me, his spiritual search turned sensuous, and I would nearly weep with jealousy and desire, the words fading on the page before me. Where could I be safe from the fragrant, furious presence of that wild young woman whom I both adored and loathed? A raw little American bitch who could scarcely read; how had I allowed her to shred me apart like this when, a star student, I already knew so much more about everything than she did? Except sex; the sharp perfume of her young, hot body rose in my nostrils, until like a maddened monk plagued by noonday visions of lewdness, I nearly swooned. I was in love with this terrible young woman, in love, maybe, with the idea that I had been sent to help her. But how? I struggled for some formula of acceptance, suitable for an Ulster ascetic, an Armagh anchorite.

When I wouldn't return to the pool, she organised a trip to the real sea, to Viareggio, perhaps because I said Rilke had once stayed there. And how sweetly careful her preparations were! She had a picnic basket, with a whole cooked chicken , a flask of wine, a good cheese and ripe fruit; just like any normal sweetheart, wife or mother, organising an outing with a loved one. We bathed, and lay under a parasol, and swam again, running with linked hands into the waves. And as I fell asleep under the parasol, weary with sun and happiness, I saw her go down to dance along the strand, her private intense dance of pleasure which I had not seen for a long time.

> By the seashore
> my love dances:
> the waves press
> to kiss her feet.
>
> Phoebus Apollo,
> the sun god,
> the light bringer,
> has blessed our feast.

But before we were bouncing back to Florence again by bus, her mood had already swung back to bitterness. There was a song she kept speaking of, a song of Billie Holiday; a name, like Mondrian, which I had never heard of in Ireland. It was *Gloomy Sunday*, and it was what she called blues, based on an old Hungarian tune, adapted by the doomed black singer. It had caused so many deaths, she said, that it was sometimes called the

Hungarian Suicide Song, and it was banned by some radio stations for its melancholy. If you listened carefully you would realise that it was the lament of someone deep into drugs, for whom life was too much pain to sustain. And she told me of Lady's life, the heavy drugs, the brutal lovers; a black boy friend claimed to have met her.

At this point the seemingly endless cloud of our quarrels induced a kind of hallucinatory confusion. Did she possess some kind of radio or record player or not, an early portable phonograph? She certainly crooned the words to herself every evening in the hot darkness, as the light faded in the open window. I watched as the head I had tried to love sank lower and lower, drowning in a sadness, a thick, black gloom that resounded through those strange, husky tones, like the dark wax that wasps exude:

> Sunday is gloom–y
> My hours are slumberless.
> Dearest, the shadows
> I live with are numberless. . .

Lulled by the spell of the song, she would topple slowly sideways to the floor, asleep. Above her was the easel she no longer used much; the few half hearted attempts she had made recently reminded me of a pump or bucket trying to dredge from a long dried well. Something was terribly wrong, and I didn't know what to do about it; I was unequipped as I had been at the pool to sound the depths to which she was sinking and revive and rescue her.

In the window
daylight fails.
My love's head
also falls. . .

The ochre shade
of the walls
fades; cracks
on a grey rock.

Love once
lit the room,
is there any
way back?

VII

Towards the end of the month her money began to run out. What were we to do? Half-heartedly, I offered to change my last traveller's cheque from Cooks, the one that was supposed to bring me to Paris. She shook my offer away, partly because she understood my reluctance only too well, and also because, perhaps, she wanted us to maintain our roles. It had to be *her* money, *her* flat, if she was to keep the upper hand in our relationship: *to call the shots*, as she coarsely said. Or: *I'm not going to raid the poorbox* was another savage reply, when I tried again.

So I waited, using all my newly won training in restraint. After a day or so sucking oranges, propping her head with her fist in total, sulky silence, her features distorted, she seemed to come to some decision. She told me curtly *to stick around*, while she went to see the owner of the flat; if you could call it that, a small bare room for which she was already over-paying. She came back with him, and another, to my eyes, ancient Italian lizard, whom I had already seen in the Black Market when we went to change dollars. A typical *sensale*, behind his old-fashioned linen suit.

We sat talking for a while in pidgin English and then suddenly I felt as if there was a vacuum in the room. No one bothered to speak, all politeness was dropped as they stared at me, or rather right through me. Thick

as a root, I still got the message. I went out and wandered the endless streets, raging. Even Florence couldn't please me: the statue of David seemed brazen, brutal, like the smirks of the young Italians on their farting motor-cycles and lambrettas. At least I had a girl and didn't have to go to whores, like they did, or pester foreigners in the streets. Finally I decided to turn back: why had she driven me out for those repulsive old codgers, with their triumphant leers, like Rembrandt's *Susanna and the Elders*? Surely she would not let *them* touch her young beauty? I felt as protective as Galahad, wrathful as Savonarola.

She was cleaning up the place when I got back. She had borrowed a broom from our surprised neighbour, and was wielding it well, with all our clothes, belongings tidied into a corner, and the only carpet hanging through the open window. I came in slowly, spotted that my rucksack was still on its peg, and sat on the bed to be out of her way. It had been made, which was not usual, with the sheet tucked under the pillow.

'What happened?' I stammered finally, when she slowed down. She did not answer so I waited until she sat down, on the only place she could, on the bed next to me.

'What h-h-happened?' I tried again. 'I ought to know. I-I want to know what they did.'

She turned her face towards me, blank at first, that deliberate blankness I had come to know so well, which baffled and troubled me. Then a rising anger sharpened her features, made her blue eyes blaze.

'So you want to know, Mr Irishman, Mr James Joyce the Second, the budding poet. A little unwashed priestly prick is more like it. Well, you can hear my confession, you pious little bastard. They wanted to fuck me, the old farts, but they'd be too afraid, too afraid of heart attacks, too afraid of mama. So they just felt me up – '

Dumb, head down, angry at her, sad for her, ashamed of myself I listened. There was no escape from, no recourse for what I was hearing.

'Yeah, they felt me up, good and plenty. One stuck his fingers up, while the other mauled my breasts. Then they changed around, like a ball game. You're shocked, aren't you, little Mr Know-It-All from Nowheresville? Maybe I even liked it better than your fumbling. My nipples hardened, anyway.'

The anger was subsiding in her voice; that strange sadness again.

'The owner spotted that of course, and the bastard stopped. He said I was a bad girl and should be punished.'

At last I was indignant. 'Surely, you didn't let them?'

'Did I what? We needed the money, didn't we?' She turned to face me, on the bed.

'Yeah, I let them spank me a bit and tickle me with the ruler but the bruises won't show. And now we needn't worry about the rent. And look under that pillow; we'll be able to eat out tonight.'

And so we did, splendidly, under a trellis lit with tiny coloured lanterns. We had melon and *prosciutto*, *bistecca alla fiorentina*, and pints of Chianti. As we made our way back she staggered: she had been talking volubly about her family, how her father didn't love her mother any more, and had been 'fucking around', of her admiration for her brother, 'who was going to be a great painter, you'll see,' but was probably bent.

'But he had the prettiest boy friends,' she said, 'I wish he'd pass them on to me. I wouldn't even mind climbing in with them: I love my brother, damn it. I hope he doesn't kill himself.'

As she cried out the last sentence people turned to look after us in the street. At first she didn't notice, launched into her monologue.

'But they don't notice the kid sister. Only the old geezers come sniffing after me. Especially in Europe – everyone's so hung-up over here.'

And then she saw the shock and amusement of the passer-bys, who skirted us, as I propped her along: a drunken young girl was not a normal sight in Italy. 'Fucking Italians,' she screamed, turning to give them the finger. 'Why don't you go and get laid at home, you greasy creeps. You fawning fuckers.'

There were two theatrically dressed *carabinieri* at the end of the street, and I didn't want them to spot her: I had already some experience of the hatred Italian police could show to visitors who got out of hand: in every hostel there was someone who had a grim story. Besides, at long last here was a situation I was familiar with. I held her up as straight as I could, hauled her up the stairs, and when she lurched towards the bed I

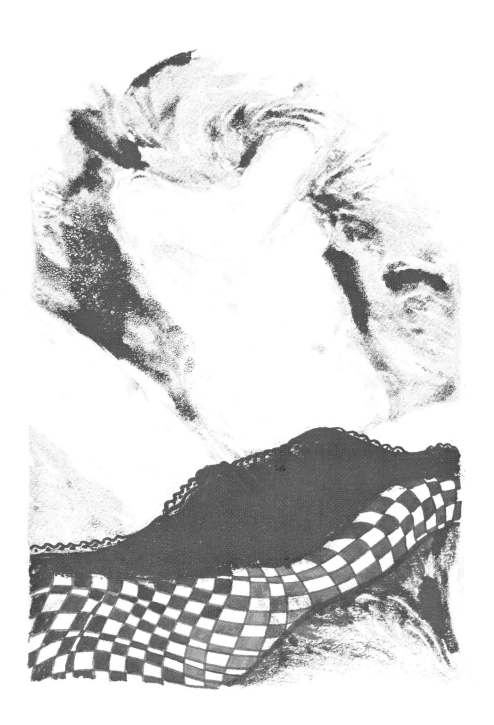

helped her to undress, the now crumpled skirt and silk stockings she wore for special outings, to get into churches and restaurants, posing briefly as a modest American miss.

Slack and vulnerable she lay across the bed, drunken mirth slowly breaking down into something even deeper than her usual sadness. Desperation, perhaps? 'They'll be back, of course, the greasy bastards, old meatballs! They know what I am, they know they can do anything with me. For them I'm just a juvenile with hot pants, a little American whore. And maybe they're right. Anything goes –.' She began to cry, a shallow stream that soon made her features ugly, nearly old. 'But you don't know who I am. And you never will.' And again she crooned:

> Sunday is gloom—y
> with shadows I spend it all.
> My heart and I
> Have decided to end it all.

That night I tried to hold her gently, to console her, but she kept pushing my hands away, as if I was molesting her. 'Go away, go away,' she cried, from the depths of her offended youth. 'Leave my tits alone, they're mine, damn you, they're mine!' As she turned and moaned in the hot night, I lay awake beside her. I was at sea, out of my depth completely. I liked what I could understand of her, the childish eagerness when she saw something beautiful, clapping her hands before a Botticelli, doing her little dance when something I had written pleased her. But her other side frightened me.

What she called my awkward body pulsed with need, and yes, I was ashamed of it, as I had been taught to be, in the gloomy corridors of school. 'Take your hands out of your pockets, boys,' rang out the Dean's reprimand. Or in the intimate dark of the confessional: 'Remember, don't defile your body, the temple of the Holy Ghost.' But I was anxious to get rid of all that shame, to be free. Until I was I couldn't help her, and I was beginning to be afraid of her games, those emotional snakes and ladders that exhausted me.

That evening she had taken our Notebook and scrawled furiously in it; what had she drawn? As she snored slightly into dawn, eyes and hair matted with tears and sweat, and the air cooled a little, I looked at the last pages. There was a scrawl of bodies, pricks and cunts coarsely entangled, in a blind ritual of defilement. She had given the sequence of squirming bodies a title which I could just make out: SEX IS SHIT.

VIII

Next morning, I made my ultimate throw. Insular and ignorant I might be, but things were adding up in my dim mind. And I was desperate for her good will. I went with my passport and last traveller's cheque to a bank and when she woke up (came to was more like it, rubbing blears from her swollen eyes) a warm breakfast was waiting.

She munched in silence and I let her be, knowing a little about the dull throb of a hangover. As she brushed the crumbs away, I ran the dishes under the sink, and then came over to stand by the bedside. She looked at me with a new, strange expression, a blend of pleading hangdog and weary defiance. I knelt by the bedside and took her lovely head in my hands. She began to weep again.

I slid in beside her, and parting the long matted coils of her hair, rocked her like a child, my hands around her shoulders. She still did not speak, and with slow hunger, my hands moved down towards the warm mounds of her breasts. As I grasped them her tears began to flow down, thick and fast. As she cried and cried, I grew wilder, pinching the rising spikes of her nipples, drinking her tears like a lapdog. Then I drove my tongue into her mouth, tasting the coppery tang of stale wine.

At long last, the tables were turned. So often that

month she had taunted and tormented me, for my awk-
wardness, for my smell even. 'You stink like a dog,' she
would say, wrinkling her nose in mock disgust: 'don't
Irish men know how to wash their groins?' Now,
broken and uncertain, she lay at my mercy, accepting
if not returning my hectic, blind advances as I forged
and foraged my way. Most of what I did she had reluc-
tantly taught me herself; instead of the slow lingering
lip kisses of Hollywood, the probing language of the
tongue, moving from one orifice to another, the mouth,
the navel, the soft nest of the quim.

At times during my apprenticeship she had
frightened me with her intensity, reaching out for me
again and again, where I lay weary and empty: 'come
on, little worm'. And when she had ruthlessly drained
me, she thrust my head down between her thighs, rubbing my face against her warm, moist fur until I choked.
Now I licked and drove like a madman, my whole body
in a fury of sensual release; emotional revenge. She
might not like it, but her body did, as whimpering she
came, with harsh cries almost like pain, her limbs shud-
dering, her body spreadeagled like a starfish, under-
neath mine. But I still held my fire, hoarded my spunk,
waiting by instinct for some last ritual of defilement.
She was so wide open now that I slid in and out of her,
with a wet smack like a second kiss.

I stopped at one point, to find her eyes watching me,
not bold anymore but the eyes of a frightened young
girl, pleading for release, and I felt like a hunter, hover-
ing near his prey. But I was still not satisfied: a mad

energy of resentment burned in me, as though I was waging war against some ghostly antagonist who stood between us, that someone who had first discovered and used this body for his own purposes. Move by move, I was tracking him down, perhaps even becoming him, in order to displace, drive him away for ever – destroy him, if necessary.

Suddenly I flipped her over, and parted her legs. I mounted her, as she had taught me, she raised her buttocks obediently, a small hand reaching out to press my hangings. But instead of the usual entrance, her rosy cleft, I probed, then sank, like a bayonet, into the folds of her arse. Deep in her fundament I finally relaxed, and the seed poured. She cried out.

We lay side by side, in silence, afterwards. 'Is that what your brother did to you?' I asked at last.

She nodded, through tears.

'Then tell me about it,' I commanded.

IX

As she talked, I saw a large house somewhere in the country outside New York, perhaps Long Island or Connecticut, the kind of comfortable barn I had seen in so many films. Her mother was a chronic amateur decorator, always busy with some new plan for the house. Her father was away, most of the time, working in New York. He took the commuter train from a nearby station, most mornings, and returned, at cocktail time. It was the rhythm of her childhood, mother fixing a pitcher of martinis before going to fetch Daddy at the station, when he had not rung to say that he was staying overnight in New York. It seemed a conventional picture; strange only to me in its assumption of continually replenished riches.

Then, in her mid teens, her parents began to quarrel. She would waken to the sound of raised, angry voices, broken glass, and later, blows and cries. She knew her elder brother would be awake too, lying and listening, so one night, when she was tired crying alone, she tippytoed down to his room. He always slept naked and it was comforting to snuggle against his warm length, leaner but larger than her teddy-bear. She came back the next night again, and they lay huddled together, listening to the warring voices below; clinging to each other like babes in the wood, as the tall trees lashed and roared.

Absorbed in their deadly fight, their parents noticed nothing. Then one night, something happened; as she lay in her brother's arms, secure and warm from the frightening sounds, that senseless screeching, she felt his groin grow large and warm against hers. Silently, in the darkness, he began to move into her. She had played naughty games with highschool boys, her mouth sore from kisses, her neck and arms covered with lovebites. But this was in a different league: her brother was seven years older than her, and already a young adult, who had made his own sexual choices, sought his own world of escape.

Although he loved his sister, and tried to defend his mother whose taste amused him, he had little or no sexual interest in women, was indeed, already a practising homosexual. So while he showed her how it was done, and let her handle him, he did not care to satisfy the wild cravings he now aroused; took pleasure, maybe, in thwarting them, preoccupied with his own revenges. Whatever he might do for her, it had to end with her sucking him or accepting to be buggered. It was what happened with his boyfriends, of course, but he also told her that it would keep her from getting pregnant.

For three years they had gone on like that, until their parents were separated, and the house was sold. By then she was nineteen, and although she dated boys at college, she found them too naive to understand her needs; their pawings seemed grotesque. Her relationship with her brother still held her, a guilty secret, and she would slip away to see him, as often as she could.

She loved him completely but when she stayed overnight in his studio loft in lower Manhattan he would
rarely sleep with her, although he was still glad to see
her. Instead, he used her as bait to attract older men
from Uptown; gallery owners, dealers and the like. He
was determined to make a name for himself as a
painter, and she was glad to be able to serve him, for
she admired him completely, he was her lord and
master. So sleeping with other men who could help him
was a bit like sleeping with him; she would tell them
about him and his work, sometimes pass them along,
if he fancied them, as he did one marvellous black jazz
musician. That had been hard but she would do anything for him as long as he would let her stay by his
side. Their father paid for art school and the rent of the
loft but her brother hated him. He blamed him for the
breakup and for their mother's unhappiness and looked
forward to when he could move away, make it on his
own.

And he had, with a good first show, and a contract
afterwards. But then something horrible had happened. Usually his boyfriends had liked her, treated her
like a mascot, and let her hang around, being helpful,
making little meals, cups of coffee. It made a pathetic
little scene, a young girl sitting studiously beside her
brother as he painted, waiting for him to throw a word
her way, a stray among the fairies. There was a little
blonde boy from Cleveland, Ohio, however, who only
pretended to be her friend, and schemed to get rid of
her, tittletattling about things she had said and done.

And when he moved in to live with her brother, she was not allowed to stay over at the flat, and even her visits became uncomfortable. He no longer needed her. One night he told her angrily that he didn't want to think about 'all that mess' anymore; he had his own life.

Neither did she, after such pain, but she couldn't find a way back to where she should be. So she asked her father to send her to Europe; she didn't know how much he suspected about her goings on but he had agreed, without conditions. He was worried about her not dating anymore and hanging around so much with his pervert son. She didn't think he was as bad as her brother did; he had a younger woman, and seemed more contented. All he asked was a postcard now and then and she had his number if anything happened her.

But Europe hadn't worked. Everything and everybody seemed so poor, so desperate; many of them didn't wash properly, and there were no showers, even proper baths. The little hotel she had stayed in London only had one bath and you had to pay extra to use it; when all the machinery got working, it was like a steam engine. And English girls had dirt under their painted fingernails and didn't know how to lay on makeup properly; they applied makeup on what was left of yesterday's. And those funny turkish toilets in France where you had to squat: it was kinda funny but after a while you felt hemmed in. And she never seemed to meet anyone young, though men followed her around everywhere, especially in Paris and Italy. As she blathered on about the shortcomings of the countries I

had just been travelling through, so excitedly, I kept pressing her for more details, for more clues.

Yes, she had had a few affairs, one with a rich creep in Milan – 'what else is there to do in that city, you can't eat the Last Supper every night!' – another with a young sailor in Sicily. 'He was so good looking, and knew how to move his body like a black boy' – that made me squirm – 'but, boy, he was boring. He wanted to come back with me to America. Imagine bringing him home to mother. He thought I was the girl equivalent of a GI meal ticket.' But in the end there was something about sex with men that had begun to disgust her: *all that rooting around*. I thought of the well known Irish street corner description of sex: *getting your hole.*

She had been picked up by an older woman when she was in Rome and had spent some good weeks with her. There was something new and different about sleeping with a woman: they understood better what it was like to be a sexual victim, used and abused. And a woman understood another woman's body whereas men were obsessed by their silly pricks, up or down, in or out. A skilful hand or tongue could do just as much; muff diving was an art.

So much for *mise*, Mr Meself, Ireland's gift to womanhood, and future star of art and love. Whether she was at long last being honest or determined to get her own back, after what I had just done, or a mixture of both, was beyond me. I had travelled farther and faster in a single month than in many years of my previous existence, trying to keep up with this sexual meteor. From cunnilingus to incest and lesbian love; if I had been looking for experience it had washed over me, nearly swamped me. We looked at each other warily, in silence. She had stopped crying.

X

We didn't last long after that. An unfinished painting stood on the easel, with a dirty towel thrown over it. And I didn't try to make love to her any more; to *bang*, as she now crudely called it, in our rare conversations. Even the weather had become murky with freakish storms that lit up our window, like a prison cell. More often than not, I lay on the floor, coming awake to harsh flashes of lightning.

And the walls of that small dingy room were beginning to feel like a prison, a narrow airless place from which I might never escape. In the end, I could take no more. Such brutal rhythms of aggression and affection were beyond me: I wanted love, yes, or at least mutual desire, but not humiliation again. I tried to explain what I felt to Wandy but she was lost in her strange torpor, a kind of pleasureless self-regard which a little Irish *schmuck* (another word she taught me) could not understand.

Neither of us talked much, neither of us wrote in the Notebook. So I resolved to leave as I had originally planned. True to form, I borrowed money from her to pay the train to Paris, although I saved part of it by hiding myself in the lavatory after the frontier, squatting determinedly while people pushed at the door. *Je suis malade, laisse moi.* And I was.

We had a last meal, in our favourite neighbourhood

restaurant. Obscurely honouring the occasion, I wore my only suit again, tie and drip dry nylon shirt. We still didn't speak much, although it was good, especially the straw covered bottle of Orvieto, I thought. 'Would you like another?' she asked timidly. 'I find it sometimes helps to be a bit drunk on trains.' And she tried to smile, that wan aftertaste of shame and gentleness which had sometimes won me back.

Impressing myself at any rate, I did not accept. Instead, we had two *stregas*, those fiery liqueurs that stir the most sluggish tongue. It was our last hour together; she in her light coloured skirt, high heels, and silk stockings, I in my brown suit, almost like adults after what was for me, at least, my first almost love affair. There was a girl waiting my return in Ireland, but if I had failed in Florence, surrounded by warmth and beauty, would I not fail again in the dripping, claustrophobic melancholy of Dublin?

Perhaps sensing my mood, she made her last play. 'Look,' she said, 'it wasn't all that bad. I know I was tough on you but I can't help it: I'm not used to having a friend, a guy of nearly my own age. I thought you just wanted to fuck me like all the others. And then drop me if the dollars dried up. Maybe you did too, a bit. But you did try to talk to me, and most of them don't. You're really the kind of pal I need, someone I can trust when I get so goddamn lonely. Maybe I could still find the way back, with your help. I was stupid and mean when I said you were awkward. You're really sensitive and sweet, a nice guy, if I'd given you more of a chance.

I promise I won't spike you again, if you stay. I'll let you love me up, all you want, if you can just wait –'

It was, for her, a long speech. And I hesitated for they were words I had longed to hear for some time. But now I didn't trust them, or myself, anymore; the protective valves of the heart had closed, I had sealed myself away from her. Was it only selfishness and was I leaving her to drown? In Paris, the tribes were beginning to gather, Donal who was hoping to meet the girl he had met on a train in Italy the previous year, Richard, the young French writer I had met in Austria, and a host of others. We would perhaps see Sartre working on a cafe terrace, *Les Deux Maggots* or round the corner, at the *Napoleon*. I could always ask her to come along: hadn't she met Gide briefly in Sicily? She might be waspish, but she was not stupid, and besides, there would soon be another cheque coming from Daddy, which would certainly help matters.

I couldn't face it: I shrank from it. I imagined us all sitting at some cafe where the young met, like the cheaper *Royal St Germain*, across the way from *Les Deux Maggots* and the *Flore*. Either she would turn on me in a tirade that would delight the more mocking of my friends or she would drop me for someone more exotic, certainly more expert, who took her fancy. Either way I would lose. I was already bruised enough to almost look forward to a period of loneliness.

My last glimpse was of her leaning against a pillar in that anonymous station. Above her head was a clock, and a sign, USCITA. She was not crying, she was not even looking, her face averted in what seemed to me now her habitual pose. It was my first adult farewell and it was a silent one. The train drew out of the station. She did not move, or wave.

> Little white flowers
> will never waken you;
> not when the black coach
> of Death has taken you.

•

Square One

Together we will undertake the extravagance of living under a sharpened conscience, in open honesty, and we will see what happens. The worst can only be catastrophe, which is better by far than a false success.

Paul-Emile Borduas

XI

Where is she now? She may well be dead, for I can not easily imagine her settling down, submitting to the routines of marriage, however well cushioned. Or if married, there would be at least one divorce, with a sullen child, like herself, growing by her side. I can see no husband; perhaps a woman friend. Or did she, like Lady, find heavy lovers on her way into the nether-world?

I don't mean to sound hostile: I admired her wildcat ferocity, and honour her glooms which were, in many ways, more excessive than any I had met, nearer the suicidal. Born a generation later, she would probably have turned to drugs, the mixture of oblivion and release she so desperately craved. And she would have moved, pitched the ante higher and higher, graduating quickly from harmless pot to hash, from LSD to mescal, coke, or heroin. Horse, scat, angel dust, nose candy, smack, scag, shit, that was her kind of language and was it her fault that she was born too early to blast herself off through some Needle Park?

We never wrote to each other, for even if we had exchanged addresses what could we have said? It became a defensive fashion amongst us not to take Americans too seriously, GI geniuses and latter-day Daisy Millers on their predictable ego trips. But if I did not love her, I certainly tried to care for her, during our short summer together, for real as well as for mercenary reasons. And if she had found my gaucheness more tolerable, I might have leap-frogged over my bleak boyhood to maturity.

Paris brought other interests, a caravan of my contemporaries slowly moving through that astonishingly energetic post-war city, from the *Mabillon* to the *Rhumerie Martiniquaise* to the *Bar Vert*, dancing at night in the cellar of the Tabou, hoping for a sight of Juliette Greco. Some people were kind to me, some were not, but I lived on my own in a high room in the Rue de Rennes, trying to decipher *La Nausée* and modern French poetry, yet crying myself to sleep at night with visions of Wandy, hugging a pillow wet with semen and tears. The Director of the Catholic Cinema Office helped me to find odd jobs, and I sought out films in remote parts of the city, romantic films like *Les Visiteurs du Soir* of Marcel Carne, Gerard Philippe in *La Chartreuse du Parme*, burying my head in their beauty. Being systematic, making an inventory, has always been my remedy for dodging sorrow and loneliness.

My dearest friend, Donal, was deeply in love with his French girl friend; they spent their days in bed, and emerged in the evening, rubbing their eyes like hibernating animals. To recover they made romantic little trips to Paris suburbs like Robinson and Chantilly. Pleased for them, but profoundly envious, I kept away, padding through the city with my red beard, khaki battle jacket and slacks, like a lean monk. It was my second time in Paris and I was determined to hold out as long as I could, undistracted by sex, dreaming of future masterworks.

I wrote a long letter to Dublin, to be read with high amusement by one young poet to another. What a provincial pattern of malice we lived in, deriding the adventures of others in search of themselves! How could they know that a young American had just taken a lump out of me, and that I was still on the injury list? Yet in spite of myself, homesickness was growing and I trudged to the Irish Embassy to read the papers and scrounge a meal from a kindly Second Secretary. Malnutrition was beginning to wear me down: we discussed repatriation.

I was locked in, miserable, a strong dose of Wandy's anguish adding to my own, all the useless ache of being young, and Irish. Finally, there was nothing for it but the long journey home, across England, two boats and a train, never sleeping, always standing, until I saw the gulls creaking over Dublin Bay. And when I got back to my digs I came down with a painful and humiliating disease, *Epididymo orchitis*, a swollen testicle. I thought the worst, of course: was this Wandy's parting shot? A kindly specialist examined me on a bench in a lecture room in the College of Surgeons, and pronounced my malady due to exhaustion. The medical students in my digs were delighted by this rare complaint and told all their contemporaries, who queued to see me. Up and down the stairs they clattered cheerfully, while our black-garbed mass-going landlady puzzled over my mysterious popularity. Disgusted, I charged a shilling

a look, which they repaid with baleful prophecies.

'If you're not sterile you'll be stuck for the rest of your life, with one ball clanging your ankles. They'll call you Chief Hanging Ball: you'll see!'

For over a week I lay in bed with it resting on a little platform of elastoplast. Only my old girl friend couldn't come to see me but I was too embarrassed to face her anyway. I could barely speak and shuffled around, like a pariah dog, waiting for the day when I could put my library up, and start to write again, in a room of my own, neither home nor boarding house. I had stopped going to church, feeling no remorse, only longing after my summer adventures. A warm picture of Wandy in my wallet meant more to me than any ikon.

And the Notebook? It stayed at the bottom of my rucksack, except when I used some of the pages to write letters, begging usually. My eldest brother sent me a cheque, with no sermon attached, although in the first flare of fear at my malady, I claimed to have caught the pox. Finally I felt so low that I went home, to my mother's house, and inflicted my torpor on my family. The *weltschmerz* of my generation, those pestiferous post-war blues had caught up with me and I never lost a chance to cast a gloom over the proceedings. Which were, God knows, gloomy enough already, with the rain falling on the narrow streets, the one cinema, the parochial hall. Still, there was a place at the table, my old bedroom, and enough pocket money to go to a local dance, though at times I wondered if I was caught again, condemned forever to the pubs and the spuds, hemmed in by holiness. On nights when I had no excuse, I knelt down to join the Family Rosary, with its long trimmings for dead relatives. My knees ached when I rose but it had begun to seem normal to be uncomfortable again.

Someone asked me for a page of writing paper and I absentmindedly tore it out for them. I then left the pad lying around; not deliberately, I had just forgotten what unIrish material it contained. A big bookshelf had been bought at an auction and I arranged my books in it: Gide, Stendhal, Balzac, Montherlant, Mauriac, only the best! I was becoming intolerable, even to myself, lurching through the small town with my burden of suffering, like a provincial genius, coming home only to eat, or endlessly read, before I fell into my solitary, Wandy haunted sleep. I woke to find the statue of the Sacred Heart in the corner staring at me; which was the real world?

I had long conversations with my mother which were like a parody of the end of Joyce's *Portrait*, with me mournfully pressing the case for freedom, and she arguing, with an equal measure of gloom, for orthodoxy though she was still capable of a pretty good thrust. When I was deploying my favourite tactic of presenting France as the eldest daughter of the Catholic Church, she scoffed: 'Everyone knows the French have low morals.' I countered with Lourdes;and the absence of any authenticated visions of the Virgin in Ireland. One of the most recent attempts had been discredited as a homemade magic lantern show, and Virgin spotting, one of the favourite sports of the pious, had been discredited for a while. There was a time when she seemed to be flashing up and down the coast of Ireland, barren plateaux in Mayo, rocky inlets in Kerry, but never nesting, to bring lustre to the crown of Ireland.

'Why has France so many saints then, mother?' I asked, innocently cute. She swatted me with ease. 'Because they need them so much more than us, son.' Then, resting in bed with a mild autumn cold, she read one of the books from my library, attracted by the title, *Pity for Women*, by Henri Montherlant. Horrified, she turned to Francois Mauriac, whom I had extolled to her as a great Catholic novelist. The novel she fell on was one of his blackest, *Le Desert de l'Amour*, the desolation of carnal love. The morality was right up my mother's alley, but the details were not.

She was so upset by this exposure to normal French culture that she hightailed it to confession, and told the priest she had been reading dirty books. Learning that she had got them from her son's library, he reproved her for prying, with what seems to me still, for the times that were in it, the prevailing moral climate, a good answer.

'He probably needs them for his study, Mrs Mac. . . A student must know all about human nature. But they could be dangerous for a quiet woman like yourself. Tell me, do you still have a subscription to *The Messenger of the Sacred Heart*?'

Coming from Father Gillfallen, whose annual sermon

comparing sexual problems with the rules of his favourite game, golf, always packed the gallery, it was a good
try. Some of his innocent injunctions had become
legends among the cornerboys. 'It all depends on how
you hold your hips, men. Too much wiggling is not
wise, if you want a clean drive.'

Or: 'Would you pick a ball up off the green when
your opponent's attention was distracted? Of course you
wouldn't but that's what an immodest touch is, stealing
a march. You don't tap the ball into the hole because
no one is looking! Respect the rules of the green and
the game will take care of itself. And this French
kissing; keep your tongue in your own mouth at all
times. A dab on the lips is more than enough – like
using the putter, gently does it. Just a flick.'

Then the Notebook disappeared. Even in my sluggish
state I registered some alarm. To any member of my
Ulster Catholic family it would almost certainly seem
obscene, indeed, to most people in Ireland at that time,
not to be unfair to my family, who were far more toler-
ant and aware than most. But the idea of it being read
by the wrong person, by someone unsympathetic to the
extreme feelings displayed in the commentary and the
drawings, the scrawls of two young people so involved
with each other, sometimes in anger, sometimes in
pleasure, filled me with rage and dismay. Perhaps they
would take it upon themselves righteously to destroy
such a sinful document; that was my worst thought,
some Manichaean dwelling upon Wandy's drawings
with puritan horror.

[93]

A few days later the Notebook or writing pad re-appeared but not where I had left it; by my bedside, on top of my Missal. Who had read it, or at least looked in it? My elder brothers? They didn't breathe a word. My uncle from Donegal, a sweet but innocent man, an ex-cleric and schoolteacher with as gentle a nature as one could meet? A few drinks was the extent of his debauchery. Once I asked him about married sex, fascinated by the idea of a semi-permanent supply. 'Ah, sure you get fashed with that too,' and when I looked puzzled, added kindly 'blow your bugle as long as you can. Marriage is the full stop.' And turned to talk of the All-Ireland Final, and the big Holy Year Cross they had raised over the town. 'You'll see it right over the Border,' he chuckled.

No one criticised me, no one chastised me, no one challenged me. And yet I felt haunted. Could someone have picked up such a document and left it down again without comment? Or somewhere in the heart of my family did someone care enough for me to contemplate what might seem to them the worst – *Com'on Baby, let's hit the sack* or *Let's stay home tonight and fuck* – and still love and cherish me enough to leave me alone? Perhaps it was my sainted mother, already thwarted by her adventures in *The Desert of Love*? It was a chastening thought – that night I dreamt of Wandy and awoke crying. I had glimpsed her, turning and twisting in a cage, a caught animal.

And I looked at the Notebook again. The poems were poor, I now knew, the lines derived from Pound or

Patchen. But some of the drawings were quite good; what began as revolt, a girl child's swollen dream of sex, endless cunt and everlasting balls, had worn itself out quickly, becoming something else. What she had been trying to paint, in faithful imitation of Piet Mondrian and his disciple, her dominating brother, had nothing to do with her real self, which was wilder, more wilful, less perfect. In her scrawls, even the most obscene, there was a sense of hurt, an angry sharpness, something violated which was desperately trying to renew itself, a protest against that soiling by the world which is so much a part of growing up. And in some there was a reaching out towards ease, cartwheels of love, arms and legs linked warmly as in Indian sculpture.

Most people attain maturity within their society with some ease, a state towards which they have rightly aspired. But for others, however insatiable, even savage, their energy, all knowledge of the world is a kind of spoiling, an endless disappointment. Her drawings reflected that intense state, an angry disruption at being born into some place and time which could not immediately satisfy her excessive but genuine needs, as a woman, and an artist.

And I was living proof of that constrictedness, alas. Perhaps I could have helped her; and myself at the same time if she had trusted me. Still, the idea that someone should look at our joint efforts with censorious eyes was almost a sacrilege. Love or lust, loathing or friendship, it was ours, a thrusting from our so differing worlds towards freedom, towards ease. What happened between us was a stumbling towards something without which two equal beings cannot survive, something called honesty. As I tidied the Notebook away carefully, I thought, perhaps next summer I might hoist my small sail again.